Enough to Help

adapted by Becky Friedman

based on the screenplay "Daniel Is Big Enough to Help Dad"
written by Jennifer Hamburg

poses and layouts by Jason Fruchter

Simon Spotlight

New York   London   Toronto   Sydney   New Delhi

INSTRUCTIONS FOR GROWTH CHART:

1. Hang the chart 16 inches above the floor. If you want, you can use this book to help you measure. It's 16 inches wide when opened! Open book and place this edge on the floor. Then the top edge of the book will be 16 inches high.

2. Each time you measure your child, you can write your child's name and age directly on the poster!

3. As your child grows, ask him or her what he or she is big enough to do and write it on the chart.

SIMON SPOTLIGHT
An imprint of Simon & Schuster Children's Publishing Division
1230 Avenue of the Americas, New York, New York 10020
First Simon Spotlight edition January 2015
© 2015 The Fred Rogers Company
All rights reserved, including the right of reproduction in whole or in part in any form.
SIMON SPOTLIGHT and colophon are registered trademarks of Simon & Schuster, Inc.
For information about special discounts for bulk purchases, please contact Simon & Schuster
Special Sales at 1-866-506-1949 or business@simonandschuster.com.
Manufactured in the United States of America 0515 LAK
10 9 8 7 6 5 4
ISBN 978-1-4814-2942-9
ISBN 978-1-4814-2943-6 (eBook)

"Hi, neighbor!" said Daniel Tiger. "Just wait until you see what my dad is doing. Follow me!"

In the backyard, Dad Tiger was building Daniel a playhouse.

"It looks just like our house!" said Daniel, giggling. "Except it doesn't have a door."

"I'm going to put the door on with my hammer," said Dad.

"Can I use the hammer?" asked Daniel.

"I'm sorry, Daniel," replied Dad. "A hammer is a grown-up tool."

"I'm not big enough to help build my playhouse," said Daniel sadly.

"Everyone is big enough to do something," said Dad. "And you are big enough to be my helper tiger and hold the door in place while I hammer."

"I can do that!" said Daniel.
Bang, bang, bang went the hammer as Daniel helped Dad.

"All done!" said Dad. "Now there's something else you're big enough to do. You can try out the door to make sure it works."

"I can do that!" said Daniel.

Open and shut, open and shut, open and shut went the door.

"Now it's time to paint the door," said Dad.
"Am I big enough to help?" asked Daniel.
"Yes!" said Dad. "Can you help me pick the paint colors?"
"I can do that!" said Daniel as he picked red, blue, and yellow paint.

"I'll paint the top of the door, and you paint the bottom," said Dad. "Deal?"

"Deal," answered Daniel.

Swish, swish, swish went the paintbrushes as Daniel helped Dad.

Daniel loved painting. He imagined he could paint with his hands . . .

"Time to put on the doorbell," said Dad. "I have to use my screwdriv[er]
"Can I use the screwdriver?" asked Daniel.
"I'm sorry, Daniel," said Dad. "A screwdriver is a grown-up tool."
"Does that mean I can't be your helper tiger anymore?" asked Daniel.

First, Dad asked
for a pencil.
"Pencil!" said
Daniel as he
handed it to Dad.

Then, Dad asked for glue.
"No glue!" said Daniel.
"Uh-oh," said Dad. "We
need the glue to put the
doorbell on the playhouse."
"I'll find it!" said Daniel.
"I'm big enough to do that!"

Daniel looked in the kitchen for the glue, and he found his mom. She was using the glue!

"Will you help me?" asked Mom Tiger. "I need to glue a handle on this cabinet."

"Okay," said Daniel.

"Whoops!" said Mom. "I dropped the handle! Where did it go?"
Daniel watched as the handle rolled and rolled and rolled until it stopped right under the cabinet.

"Oh no!" said Mom. "My hand is too big to reach it!"

"I'll get it!" said Daniel. "My hand is just the right size."

Daniel reached and reached and reached until . . .

Daniel finished helping Mom and then brought out the glue to Dad. "A little glue here, a twist of the screwdriver, and . . . all finished!" said Dad. "Thank you for helping me, my big helper tiger. And now, I think you are big enough to play in your new playhouse."

"I can do that!" said Daniel. He smiled proudly as he stepped inside.

Ding! Dong! Dad rang the doorbell.
"Come in!" said Daniel.
"I can't!" said Dad. "I'm too big! But this playhouse is just the right size for *YOU*."

"I like being big enough to play inside my playhouse," said Daniel Tiger. "Everyone is big enough to do something. What are *YOU* big enough to do? Ugga Mugga!"